MERCER MAYER'S
LC +THE CRITTER KIDS®

THE
SECRET CODE

A Golden

Western Publishing Comp............................04

A Mercer Mayer........[...]. R. Sansevere book

Library of Congress Catalog Card Number: 93-73763
ISBN: 0-307-15983-3/ISBN: 0-307-65983-6 (lib. bdg.) A MCMXCIV

Written by Erica Farber/J. R. Sansevere

LC

VELVET

LITTLE SISTER

TIGER

KOOL BEAR

SLICK RICK

SU SU GABBY TIMOTHY

GATOR FLEX HENRIETTA

CHAPTER 1

DR. MOLE'S DASTARDLY DUNGEON

LC jumped up from his seat as soon as the bell rang. Then he pulled something out from under his desk. He put it on top of his books.

He ran toward his locker. His two best friends, Tiger and Gator, were already there.

"Hey, dude, you got it!" Tiger said.

"Yep," said LC.

"Wow!" Gator said. "My brother and his friends have been looking for it all over Critterville."

"It was really cool of your uncle to send it

to you," Tiger said. "Awesome!"

LC's Uncle Andy lived in the city, and he always sent the best presents. But this was the best present ever. LC hadn't even opened it yet. He was waiting until he and his friends were at their clubhouse so they could all open it together.

"My brother told me that none of his friends have made it past Level I," Gator said.

"Yeah," Tiger agreed. "I heard that nobody's ever made it to Level II."

"I bet we can do it," LC said.

All three stared at the small cardboard box in LC's hand. It said DR. MOLE'S DASTARDLY DUNGEON, GAME II. It was the latest video game, and everybody wanted to play it.

"I'll take that," a deep voice said. Suddenly a fat hand grabbed the box away from LC.

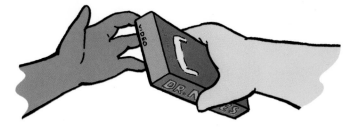

Flex, the bully of Critterville Elementary, held the game high up in the air. Flex was older and bigger. He was also mean.

"Hey, that's mine," LC said.

"Not anymore," Flex said, waving the game in the air. "I've been looking for this game."

"Give it back," Tiger said, jumping up to grab the game.

Flex just laughed and began to open the box.

"Hey, there's no game in here," Flex said, shaking the box. "This is bogus."

Flex threw the empty box at LC and walked off down the hall. LC picked up the

box. Flex was right—the box was empty.

"What happened to the game?" Gator asked.

"Yeah," said Tiger.

"Somebody took it," said LC. "And I think I know who."

"Who?" Tiger and Gator both asked.

"Follow me," said LC.

LC, Tiger, and Gator took off down the hall. They ran down the front steps of the school and around the corner, smack into Gabby and Su Su. The girls both dropped their books.

"Hey!" Gabby and Su Su yelled at the boys. But Tiger, Gator, and LC didn't stop.

"I don't know what the big rush is," said Su Su. "I mean, they're probably just on their way to their stupid clubhouse. They act like their club is such a big deal."

"Really," agreed Gabby, standing up.

"What do they do in their clubhouse anyway?" Su Su asked.

"Trade baseball cards and play video games,"

Gabby said, picking up one of her books.

"Bor-ing," said Su Su.

"I know," Gabby said. "I mean, clubs ought to be for doing important stuff."

"Yeah," Su Su agreed. She reached down to pick up the other book Gabby had dropped.

"*The Mystery of the Critterville Clock*," Su Su said, handing the book to Gabby. "You're still reading Nancy Critter mystery stories?"

"Well, yeah," Gabby said. Gabby loved Nancy Critter, and she wanted to be a famous detective like Nancy Critter more than anything.

"And actually, I was thinking of starting a detective club," Gabby said. Gabby thought she and Su Su would make excellent detectives.

"Puh-leaze!" Su Su said. "Detective clubs are for babies. The only club I'm join- ing is the Critter Golf and Tennis Club." Before Gabby could say another word, Su Su took off down the block.

Gabby was mad. She couldn't believe Su Su didn't want to be in her detective club. She thought the detective club was the best idea she'd ever had. Gabby walked home slowly, trying to figure out who could be in her detective club. A club couldn't have just one person in it.

At that moment LC, Tiger, and Gator were in LC's backyard, heading for the clubhouse.

It was really an old barn, but LC and his friends had made it into their clubhouse. LC slid open the big wooden door and there, sitting in his favorite chair, was Little Sister. And just as he suspected, she was playing his new game.

"Give me that game," LC said, walking over to his sister.

"Guess what?" Little Sister said, her eyes glued to the TV set. "I already made it to Level VII. I killed Frankengator. On Level V, I sucked all the blood out of Dracuduck. And now I have enough juice to destroy Dr. Mole and blow up his dastardly dungeon."

LC, Tiger, and Gator stared at Little Sister.

Suddenly the screen exploded with color. Little Sister had destroyed Dr. Mole and blown up his dungeon. She had won the game.

"Awesome!" Tiger said, putting his shoe-box full of baseball cards on the table.

"You stole my game," LC said.

"Did not," Little Sister said, throwing

down the controls. "I just borrowed it."

LC grabbed the controls and began to play. If Little Sister could destroy Dr. Mole, so could he.

"Got anything to eat?" Tiger asked.

"Excellent brownies," Gator mumbled.

He was already eating one of the double chocolate chip peanut butter fudge brownies Mrs. Critter had made. They were on the table in the middle of the room.

LC nodded at his friends, but he didn't

look up from the game. He was determined to destroy Frankengator and get to Level VII.

Little Sister grabbed a brownie off the plate on the table and stuffed it in her mouth. She loved brownies, especially double chocolate chip peanut butter fudge ones. Then she went over to LC.

"You're running out of power," Little Sister said through a mouthful of brownie. Some crumbs fell onto LC's shoulder. "You just passed the power pack. You should have picked it up."

"Where? I don't see a power pack," LC said.

"It's behind the rock," Little Sister said, taking another big bite of brownie. "You're dead."

"I am not," LC said.

Just then Frankengator killed LC's guy.

GAME OVER flashed on the screen.

"It's all your fault," LC said. "I was doing great until you came."

"Great?!" Little Sister said. "You weren't even on Level II."

"What are you doing here?" LC said, putting down the game.

"Mom said I could have a brownie," Little

Sister said. "Anyway, you guys are no fun!" With that, she grabbed the last brownie and stomped out of the barn. She slid the door shut with a bang.

LC went over to the table where Tiger and Gator were putting out their comics and cards. Suddenly there was a knock at the door. It wasn't just one knock, it was a series of knocks with strange pauses in between.

"Come in!" LC yelled.

"Come in?!" someone yelled back from the other side of the door. "But I didn't give you the secret code."

"Hey, that sounds like Gabby," Tiger said, going over to open the door.

Gabby walked inside, carrying a paper bag filled with stuff. "So what's your secret code?" she asked.

"We don't have a secret code," LC said.

"Well, you should," Gabby said. "Every club has to have a secret code."

"Why?" Gator asked.

"Because . . . just because," Gabby said,

dropping her bag on the table and scattering the baseball cards and comics. "Anyway, what do you guys do in your club?"

LC looked at Tiger. Tiger looked at Gator. Gator looked at LC. "Stuff," LC finally said.

"Stuff?!" Gabby exclaimed. "Real clubs don't just do stuff. Real clubs have goals. And . . . and . . . do important things. But don't worry. I know just how to make our new club into a *real* club."

"What kind of real club?" LC asked.

Gabby didn't answer. Instead, she grabbed her bag and went over to the blackboard in the corner of the room.

All eyes were on her as she picked up a piece of chalk and wrote:

THE CRITTER KIDS' DETECTIVE CLUB

"Look, I've got all the stuff we need," she said, pulling things out of her bag. "Starting with baby powder."

"Baby powder?" Tiger said. "I thought you said this was a detective club, not a baby-sitting club."

"Baby powder is for dusting for fingerprints," Gabby said. "And look at all this other stuff. A pen that is really a flashlight. And a magnifying glass for examining clues. And a stamp pad for taking fingerprints. I think we should start by taking everybody's fingerprints."

Gabby grabbed LC's thumb and shoved it

onto the ink pad. Black ink oozed all over his hand. Then she pushed his hand onto a piece of paper and mashed it around for a minute.

"After we're done with the fingerprinting, we have to invent a secret code for sending messages," Gabby said, picking up Tiger's hand and putting one of his fingers on the ink pad. "That way we can tell each other secrets at school without anyone else knowing. Isn't that gonna be great?"

LC didn't answer. But he couldn't help thinking that this detective stuff was only going to lead to one thing—trouble.

CHAPTER 2

A NEW FOX IN TOWN

The next morning in social studies, LC was sitting at his desk in the third row. There was a new girl sitting right next to LC. "Hello," LC said to the new girl. But she didn't say hello back.

"Before we start our lesson today," began Mr. Hogwash, "I would like to introduce a new member of our class, Velvet Fox."

The girl next to LC shifted in her seat and stared at the floor.

"Velvet, where are you from?" Mr. Hogwash asked.

"The city," Velvet said so quietly that only

LC could hear her.

"Where?" Mr. Hogwash asked.

"The city," Velvet mumbled again, her eyes still glued to the floor.

"We can't hear you, Velvet," Mr. Hogwash said.

"The city!" LC yelled. "She said she's from the city."

Velvet Fox suddenly looked up from the floor and gave LC a tiny smile.

"Well, thank you, Mr. Critter," Mr. Hogwash said. Then he began to talk about the civilization of ancient Egypt. LC started drawing pictures of pyramids.

Just then a note landed on LC's desk. He opened it slowly. The note was in Gabby's handwriting, but LC had no idea what it said because it was written in the secret code Gabby had made up. LC flattened the note on his desk and stared at it.

When Mr. Hogwash turned to write on the blackboard, LC reached into his desk and took out the master code sheet Gabby had made. She had told them to tear it into tiny pieces after they memorized it. Otherwise, spies might find it and then they would know the code. The thing was, LC hadn't quite memorized the code yet.

"Does anyone know what hieroglyphics are?" Mr. Hogwash asked the class.

LC squirmed in his seat. He hadn't read all of the section on ancient Egypt in his text-book, and he hoped Mr. Hogwash wouldn't call on him. But Mr. Hogwash had this weird way of knowing exactly who knew the answer and exactly who didn't—and he

loved to call on anyone who didn't.

"LC, do you know what hieroglyphics are?" Mr. Hogwash asked. He walked over to LC's desk.

"Um . . . er . . . I . . . um . . ." LC mumbled.

"Ah, what have we here?" Mr. Hogwash said, reaching down for the note Gabby had sent LC. "A message written in code."

Before LC knew what he was doing, he shoved the master code sheet into his mouth. He couldn't let Mr. Hogwash have the code. Gabby would kill him. There was nothing else to do—LC just had to eat it.

Lucky for LC, Mr. Hogwash did not notice the big lump in LC's mouth.

"How clever, Mr. Critter," Mr. Hogwash said as he stared at LC's message. "You see, the ancient Egyptian language of hieroglyphics is like a secret code for us today. We must learn their symbols and crack their code in order to understand what the Egyptians have written."

LC chewed the paper as fast as he could until it turned into a mushy blob. He hoped Mr. Hogwash wouldn't ask him another question until he had swallowed it.

"Why don't we try to crack Mr. Critter's secret code," Mr. Hogwash said, smiling down at LC. "I'll write it on the board and we can all try and figure it out."

LC swallowed the note in one gulp. It tasted terrible.

Gabby turned around and glared at him. He slumped down farther in his seat as Mr. Hogwash copied the note onto the board:

M22T Y45 3N TH2 CL5BH45S2
1T 01500 H45RS

"That's easy," Timothy said, raising his hand. "Obviously, the numerals 1-2-3-4-5 stand for letters, and the letters stand for just what they are—letters. Let's see. There are five numbers used here, which corresponds exactly to the number of vowels in the English alphabet. So if you figure that the letter **A** is **1**, **E** is **2**, **I** is **3**, **O** is **4**, and **U** is **5**, then we should be able to read this message quite easily."

"Excellent, Timothy," Mr.

Hogwash said. "Perhaps since this is Mr. Critter's message, he would like to have the honor of writing it out on the board."

LC got up slowly from his desk and began the long walk to the front of the room. He wished the floor would open up and swallow him.

"Well, Mr. Critter, are you ready to begin?" Mr. Hogwash said, handing LC a brand-new piece of yellow chalk.

M, LC printed, squeaking the chalk.

"Ouch!" Su Su said from the front row. "Don't you know how to use chalk?"

Now, what was **2** again? LC thought. **A** was **1**, so **E** was **2**. That meant the first word was **MEET**. LC hoped Gabby hadn't written anything too embarrassing.

"Very good, Mr. Critter," Mr. Hogwash said.

In a few minutes LC had spelled out all of the message except for the very end. It said MEET YOU IN THE CLUBHOUSE AT **01500** HOURS. LC couldn't figure the **01500** part out.

"**01500** means three o'clock," Timothy said. "It's military time."

"Excellent, Timothy," Mr. Hogwash said.

LC walked back to his seat. He was really glad that was over.

After school LC went to his locker to get his books. He hoped that Gabby would forget about all this secret code stuff since everybody in school knew the code now.

LC opened his locker door as slowly as possible. But it was no use. Books, papers, gym clothes, comic books, and notebooks fell out. He stuffed everything back inside, and suddenly noticed a pink envelope with his name on it. He wondered what it could be. Maybe it was a party invitation.

He slid open the envelope. Inside was a

piece of pink paper with something written on it. And the something was written in code. LC couldn't believe it. This code was even stranger-looking than the other code. Gabby must have already made up a new code.

LC shoved the note and his books into his knapsack and walked down the hall. He hoped he wouldn't run into Gabby.

When LC got to the playground, Tiger and Gator were shooting hoops. And Gator was winning.

Gabby and Henrietta were standing by the

basketball court. They were talking and pretending not to watch the boys. Just then Gator sank another basket.

"Hey! I've got the winner!" Henrietta yelled.

"Sorry, Henrietta," said Tiger. "We've got a club meeting."

Gator, Tiger, and LC all hated playing one-on-one against Henrietta. She was the queen

of the slam dunk at Critterville Elementary.

"I've got band practice anyway," Henrietta said, picking up her trumpet case. "See you guys later."

Just then a long black limo pulled up in front of the school. A critter dressed all in black got out and opened the back door.

"Whoa! Nice wheels!" Tiger exclaimed.

"Wonder whose car that is," Gabby said.

"Don't know," said Gator.

At that moment Velvet Fox came out of the school building. She walked toward the car. She looked over at LC and his friends for a second before she was pulled into the back-seat of the car by someone inside. The critter in black slammed the door shut behind her. He stared across the

playground at Gabby, Tiger, Gator, and LC. Then he straightened his black cap and climbed behind the wheel. He gunned the engine, and the limo pulled out of the parking lot.

"There's something strange going on here," Gabby said, her eyes following the limo.

"I think this detective stuff is going to your head," LC said to Gabby.

"Then how do you explain this?" Gabby said, holding up a pink note written in code exactly like the one LC had found in his locker.

"You got one, too?!" Gator and Tiger both exclaimed.

LC didn't say anything. He just pulled his pink note out of his knapsack.

CHAPTER 3

WHODUNIT?

LC, Tiger, Gator, and Gabby were sitting around the clubhouse table. In front of them were the four notes they had gotten. They were all exactly the same.

"I don't think that code is English," Tiger said.

"Maybe it's Transylvanian," Gator said.

"Yeah," Tiger said. "Maybe a vampire sent the notes."

"Puh-leaze," Gabby said. "Will you get serious?"

"I think it's even weirder than that," LC

said. "I bet it's hieroglyphics."

"We're not getting anywhere," Gabby said. "Let's make a list of suspects."

"Why?" Tiger asked.

"Because that's what Nancy Critter always does," Gabby said. "And Nancy Critter always solves her cases."

Gabby walked over to the blackboard. She picked up the chalk and turned toward the window. "Do you feel like we're being watched?" she whispered suddenly.

"Don't be silly, Gabby," said LC. "Why would anybody want to watch us?"

Gabby shrugged and turned back to the board as a shadow moved closer to the win- dow.

She wrote:

SUSPECT #1 SU SU

"Su Su?" Tiger said. "Why would Su Su send us these notes?"

"Because Su Su really wants to be in our detective club," Gabby said. "She just can't admit it."

"No way!" Tiger, Gator, and LC said at the same time.

"All right, then you think of a suspect," Gabby said, putting her hand on her hip.

"Mr. Hogwash!" LC said.

"Mr. Hogwash?" Gabby said. "Give me a break."

"No, I really think it's Mr. Hogwash," LC said. "He's trying to teach us a lesson for passing notes in class."

"Mr. Hogwash would never use pink paper," Gabby said.

LC, Tiger, Gator, and Gabby spent the next hour making a list of suspects. By the time they were finished, the entire blackboard was covered with names. They had listed almost everyone in their class. And they were no closer to solving the case.

Just then there was a loud crash. It sounded like it was just outside the window.

"What was that?" Tiger asked.

"Let's go look," LC said, trying to sound braver than he felt. He crept slowly over to the window. Tiger, Gator, and Gabby were right behind him. He inched his head up toward the glass, and he took a deep breath.

"Did you look?" Gabby asked, her eyes shut tight.

"Not yet," LC said. "I'm about to."

"Go for it, dude," Tiger said.

"We're right behind you," Gator said.

Finally LC stuck his head up and looked out the window. What he saw made him burst out laughing.

"What's so funny?" Gabby asked.

"Look and see," LC said, motioning for

everybody to look out the window.

Right below the window were two buckets and one of Little Sister's hair ribbons. They all watched as Little Sister ran back to the house.

"Little Sister," Tiger said.

"Yup," said LC.

"See, I was right," Gabby said. "I told you somebody was watching us. Now back to business."

"Come on, Gabby," Tiger said. "Didn't we do enough for one day?"

"Yeah," agreed Gator and LC.

"Nope," said Gabby. "Our job isn't over until our case is solved."

All four of them went back to the table. LC picked up one of the pink notes. They had to solve this mystery soon before Gabby got them into a big mess.

CHAPTER 4

RED ALERT

That night LC went to bed almost as soon as he finished his homework. Solving a mystery was hard work and he was tired. He fell asleep right away. . . .

LC walked to the center of the stage. He put on the power gloves that would give him the ultimate power to defeat Dr. Mole.

He turned and raised his arms

in the air. The crowd cheered. He had made it to Level VII without a single mistake and was about to compete in the National Championship Finals of DR. MOLE'S DASTARDLY DUNGEON, GAME II. *The crowd began to chant his name:* "LC . . . LC . . . LC . . ."

LC jolted awake. It was the middle of the night. He wasn't at the Dr. Mole finals. And the crowd wasn't chanting his name. He was at home in his bed. And Gabby's voice was calling him. It was coming out of the walkie-talkie on his table.

"Testing, testing. LC, are you there? This is an emergency," Gabby said.

LC picked up the walkie-talkie.

"This is a red alert," Gabby said. "LC, are you there?"

LC pressed the talk button. "Hi, Gabby," LC said, and yawned.

"You're supposed to say 'ten-four,'" Gabby said. "LC, don't you remember?"

"Oh, right," LC said. "Ten-four, roger, over and out, this is LC," LC said.

"LC!" Gabby yelled. "Cut it out! Listen to me. This is a red alert. There's something

strange going on at the Fox Hall Mansion. I just saw weird lights flashing on and off."

"Well, maybe they turned off the lights because they're going to bed," LC said.

"No, the lights flashed on and off," Gabby said. "I think somebody's in trouble and they're sending a signal for help. I think it's Velvet."

"Velvet?" LC said.

"Yes. Velvet Fox, the new girl in our class. I think she's been kidnapped," Gabby said. "Remember how she looked at us right before she got into the car? I bet she was trying to tell us something. And what about the critter in black? He gave me the creeps."

LC didn't say anything. It was true that Velvet was very quiet and nobody knew anything about her. And the critter in black did seem kind of strange. But still. It was the middle of the night. And Gabby's imagination was probably just running wild.

"We have to have a plan," Gabby said. "Nancy Critter always has a plan."

LC yawned. He wished Gabby would stop talking so he could go back to sleep.

"LC, I think we should go over to the Fox Hall Mansion right now and find out what's going on. We've got to get to the bottom of this."

"Gabby, I think we should wait till the morning before we do anything," LC said. "That way we can really have time to plan what we're going to do." He hoped Gabby would forget about it by then.

"But LC—" Gabby said.

"Gabby," LC said, "I bet Nancy Critter makes all her plans very carefully. I bet she never just rushes into something." LC had never read a Nancy Critter book in his life. But if he was right, then maybe Gabby would leave him alone and he could go back to sleep and continue his great dream about the Dr. Mole finals.

"That's true," Gabby said. "Nancy Critter is always prepared. So we'll get ready and go over to the Fox Hall Mansion tomorrow night to investigate."

"Hmmm," LC mumbled through a yawn. He was so sleepy all of a sudden.

"Promise, LC?" Gabby said.

"Promise," LC said.

"Good night, LC," Gabby said.

" 'Night," LC said.

LC fluffed up his pillow and pulled up the covers. Before he knew it, he was standing back onstage with the power gloves on his hands. The crowd was cheering and clapping as the master of ceremonies handed LC a big gold trophy. LC had won the finals! He was the world champion of DR. MOLE'S DASTARDLY DUNGEON, GAME II.

LC smiled in his sleep as the sun began to rise over Critterville.

CHAPTER 5

OPERATION SPRING FOX

LC looked at the clock. In one minute the bell would ring and it would be time for class. And the whole mystery of Velvet Fox would be solved when Velvet walked into the classroom. 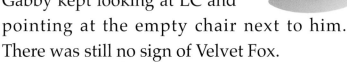 Gabby kept looking at LC and pointing at the empty chair next to him. There was still no sign of Velvet Fox.

LC knew that in exactly 30 seconds Mr. Hogwash would pick up the chalk and start the class. Mr. Hogwash didn't like to waste a single second of class time.

The bell rang. Mr. Hogwash began writing on the blackboard. "Now take out your notebooks," Mr. Hogwash said.

Just then the classroom door opened. LC looked over at Gabby with an I-told-you-so expression on his face. He knew all along that Velvet would show up.

But it wasn't Velvet. It was Nurse Robin.

"Good morning, Nurse Robin," Mr. Hogwash said.

"Good morning, Mr. Hogwash," Nurse Robin said. "I just wanted to tell you that Velvet Fox won't be in school today. Her parents called and said that she wasn't feeling very well."

LC looked at Gabby. She was writing something on a piece of paper. Maybe Gabby was right, LC thought. Maybe Velvet had been kidnapped.

Mr. Hogwash began writing on the blackboard again. A second later Gabby's note landed right on LC's desk. Gabby was great at passing notes. She never got caught.

LC slowly opened the note. This time *he* wasn't going to get caught. He held the note under his desk. Then he checked to make sure that Mr. Hogwash was still writing on the board. LC pushed back his chair so he could read the note.

Before he knew what happened, LC's chair tipped over and he landed on the floor with a loud crash. The note flew out of his hand and onto the floor. Everyone laughed.

LC sat back down as Mr. Hogwash picked up the note and looked at it.

TONIGHT CLUBHOUSE...

OPERATION SPRING FOX...

PASS IT ON

"It seems that there is a meeting at the club-house," Mr. Hogwash said. "Mr. Critter may attend, of course, but first he must make sure he has completed his one 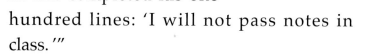 hundred lines: 'I will not pass notes in class.'"

LC groaned. He hated writing lines. Tiger and Gator gave him the thumbs-up from where they sat across the room. He had to tell them about *Operation Spring Fox*. He had a feeling that he and Gabby were going to need all the help they could get.

Later that night LC slipped out the back door of his house. He ran over to the club-

house where Gabby, Tiger, and Gator were waiting for him. Under the cover of darkness, LC and the Critter Kids spread out. LC went first. When he got to the middle of the block, he looked toward the corner. No one was in sight. He motioned to Gabby that the coast was clear. As LC ran to the next tree, Gabby moved to his tree, Tiger ran to Gabby's tree, and Gator ran to Tiger's tree.

LC shook his head. It was taking them an awful long time just to move down their block. It would take them all night to get to the Fox Hall Mansion at this rate.

Suddenly there was a loud hooting sound. Everybody ran to LC's tree.

"What was that?" Tiger asked.

"I don't know," said LC.

"Maybe we should do this tomorrow," Gator said.

"Come on, you guys, it's just an owl," said Gabby. "Let's go. We can't back out now. *Operation Spring Fox* must be carried out." Gabby grabbed the flashlight out of LC's hand and marched ahead. They all followed.

The Fox Hall Mansion was dark except for one room on the first floor. LC and the Critter Kids crept slowly toward the house. LC wondered what they were going to do next.

"Okay, guys," said Gabby. "Let's make a pyramid. LC and Tiger on the bottom. Gator on top. Remember, hold still when I climb up."

LC went down on his hands and knees in the grass. Tiger did the same. Then Gator got on top of LC. Gabby stuck her muddy

sneaker on LC's back and
climbed on top of him.

"Ow!" LC said. Gabby was pretty heavy.

"Hold still," Gabby said. "I can't get my
balance."

"I'm trying, I'm trying," LC said.

Gabby put her other foot on Gator and
moved her hands up on the windowsill.
Then she pulled herself up so that she could

see in the window.

There was a fire burning in the fireplace and lots of antique furniture. Someone was standing with his back to the window, facing the fireplace. Just then someone else moved out of the shadows. She was wearing a long evening gown.

"It's all over now," the evening gown said.

"We've got the girl, we've stolen the money, and now there's only one thing left to do."

The first figure turned around slowly. Gabby thought he looked really creepy.

"Good-bye, Charles," the evening gown said. "I'm sorry it has to be like this." With that, she pulled out a gun and aimed it at Charles.

"Oh, my gosh, she's got a gun!" Gabby shouted.

At that moment a car drove up. The headlights shone in LC's face. He moved his hand to cover his eyes, and the pyramid collapsed. LC, Tiger, Gator, and Gabby all landed in a heap on the ground.

"What have we here?" someone asked. It was the critter in black.

Nobody moved or said a word.

"Why don't you come inside and join us," the critter in black said.

The Critter Kids followed him into the house.

"Right this way," the critter in black said, pushing them into the room that Gabby had been spying on.

"Excuse me, sir, madam. We have visitors," the critter in black announced.

"Charles, you're still alive!" Gabby yelled. "She didn't shoot you!"

Charles and the figure in the evening gown looked up in surprise.

"I should hope not," Charles said. "We still have a lot more rehearsing to do."

"Rehearsing?" Gabby said, looking confused.

"Yes, our play opens next week," Charles said.

"You mean you're not kidnappers?" Gabby asked. "And you didn't kidnap Velvet Fox and steal the Fox Hall valuables?"

"I should hope not," the evening gown said. "After all, I am Mrs. Fox, this is Mr. Fox, and Velvet is our daughter. I see you've already met James, our chauffeur."

"Well, then, where's Velvet? Why wasn't she in school today?" Gabby asked.

"Velvet has a cold, so she stayed home," Mr. Fox said. "Why don't you give her a call tomorrow? She should be feeling much better by then."

Mr. Fox scribbled something on a piece of paper and handed it to LC. "Here's our phone number," Mr. Fox said.

"James, why don't you take our guests home," said Mrs. Fox. "I'm sure their parents are wondering where they are. It was nice to meet all of you and I hope to see you again soon."

LC, Gabby, Tiger, and Gator piled into the back of the limo. There was a TV, a stereo,

and headphones. "Cool!" LC said.

"You know," Gabby pointed out, "we never actually saw Velvet. And we don't really have proof that those people are her parents."

"Oh, no," LC said. "I'm not listening to any of this."

LC put on the headphones and turned on the music.

"We still don't know who sent us those notes," Gabby continued. "We better meet tomorrow at the clubhouse and get to the bottom of this mystery."

LC couldn't hear what Gabby was saying, and he didn't want to.

CHAPTER 6

OUTFOXED

The next day was Saturday, so LC, Tiger, Gator, and Gabby all met at the clubhouse early that morning. In the middle of the table were the four pink notes.

"We've still got a mystery to solve," Gabby said.

"I think we've had enough of this detective stuff," LC said.

Tiger and Gator nodded. They wanted to play video games and trade baseball cards.

"But we still have to solve the mystery of the secret code," Gabby continued.

Everyone groaned.

Just then Little Sister barged in, chewing a big piece of Bananarama gum. "I wanna play DR. MOLE'S DASTARDLY DUNGEON, GAME II," Little Sister said, blowing a big yellow bubble.

"Not now," LC said. "We're trying to figure something out."

"What?" Little Sister said. She picked up one of the pink notes. "You mean this?"

"Yes, that," LC said, grabbing it out of Little Sister's hand.

"Well, I don't know what the big deal is," Little Sister said, walking toward the door. "Somebody just wants to be your friend."

"What do you mean?" Gabby said.

"You mean you can't read the note?" Little Sister said.

All four of them shook their heads. "What are you gonna give me if I tell you?" Little Sister said.

"A baseball card," Tiger said.

"A rookie card," Little Sister said.

"Okay, tell us," Gabby said.

"What else are you going to give me?" Little Sister said.

"A pack of Bananarama gum," Gabby said.

"Ten packs," Little Sister said.

"Okay, okay," Gabby said. "Will you show us already?"

"What else are you going to give me?" Little Sister said.

"A banana split," LC said. "Come on,

Little Sister, give us a break."

"Three," Little Sister said. They nodded.

Little Sister walked back to the table, picked up one of the notes, and went over to an old mirror in the corner of the clubhouse. LC, Tiger, Gator, and Gabby all gathered around her.

Then Little Sister held the note up to the mirror. "See," she said, blowing another yellow bubble. "It says 'I want to be your friend.'"

"Wow!" the four of them said.

Little Sister shook her head and left the clubhouse.

"So the mystery is solved," Tiger said.

"Not exactly," Gabby said. "We still don't know who sent the notes."

"Oh, yes, we do," LC said.

"How do you know?" Gabby asked.

"Because they were written on the exact same pink paper that Mr. Fox gave me last night," LC said, holding up the pink paper with the Foxes' telephone number on it.

"And since Velvet is new in school, she probably just wants to be friends."

"Now what?" Gator wanted to know.

"Now we're going to call Velvet Fox and invite her over to the clubhouse," LC said.

"Wow!" said Gabby. "Pretty good detective work, LC—for a beginner anyway."

LC smiled. It felt pretty good solving a mystery.

"I'll call Velvet," said Gabby. She got up from the table and walked out the door.

"Now we can finally play DR. MOLE'S DASTARDLY DUNGEON, GAME II," Tiger said. "All right!"

"Yeah," Gator agreed, grabbing the controls.

A while later Gabby and Velvet walked into the clubhouse. Everybody cheered.

"You can play the winner," LC said to Velvet.

"Okay," Velvet said. "But I'm not very good at video games."

"What do you like to do?" Gabby asked.

"Well, I like to read Nancy Critter mystery stories," Velvet said.

"You do?" Gabby said with a big smile.

"Yeah," said Velvet. "Have you read *The Mystery of the Critterville Clock*?"

"I just finished it," said Gabby. "Wasn't it great?"

"Yeah," agreed Velvet.

"Well, you know I started this detective club," said Gabby.

"Really," said Velvet.

Uh-oh, LC thought. It looked like the Critter Kids' Detective Club was here to stay.